MOMMY,
Can We Pray for
Unicorns?

PAGE PUBLISHING, INC.
Conneaut Lake, PA

First originally published by Page Publishing 2021

ISBN 978-1-6624-4134-9 (pbk)
ISBN 978-1-6624-4135-6 (digital)

Printed in the United States of America

MOMMY, Can We Pray for Unicorns?

Sarah Dienethal

"Sydney, it's time for bed," said Mommy.

Sydney hopped up in excitement and crawled up onto the bed. "Mommy, can we pray?"

"Of course!" said Mommy. "What would you like to pray about tonight?"

Sydney thought for a moment and then asked with a smile, "Can we pray for the butterflies?"

"Of course, we can pray for the butterflies," said Mommy.

Sydney jumped up on her bed and spun in circles, flapping her arms like a butterfly. "I'll pray for them all to come back in the spring," she said excitedly. "Hundreds of them, and they will all be my best butterfly friends!"

"Mommy, can we pray for kittens too?" Sydney asked, sitting back down on her bed.

"I'm sure kittens need prayers just as much as you and me," said Mommy.

"I'll pray that *all* the lost kittens all over the world find a home!" said Sydney, beaming with excitement. "Maybe our home!"

"That's a beautiful prayer," said Mommy, tickling Sydney's tummy.

"Mommy, can we pray for unicorns?" asked Sydney with a grin.

Mommy thought for a moment. "You know, sweetie, unicorns aren't really real. Just pretend."

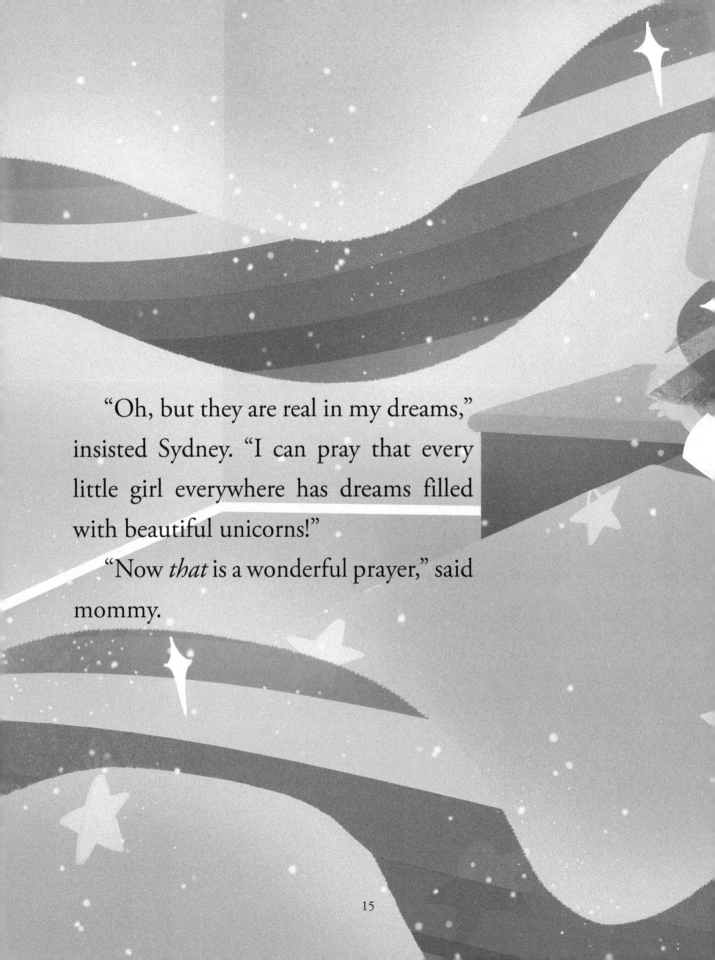

"Oh, but they are real in my dreams," insisted Sydney. "I can pray that every little girl everywhere has dreams filled with beautiful unicorns!"

"Now *that* is a wonderful prayer," said mommy.

"Mommy, can we pray for popcorn?" asked Sydney, rubbing her belly hungrily.

"Popcorn!" exclaimed mommy. "How do we pray for popcorn?"

"Everyone should get popcorn," said Sydney, jumping up and down on the bed. "I'll pray that every kid everywhere never has to go without popcorn!"

"You know," said Mommy, "those are some wonderful prayers, but did you know that prayers are also a way to say thank you for everything you already have?"

"What do you say thank you for?" asked Sydney.

"Well, I say thank you for a lot of things like our home and your teachers and our friends and grandparents," said Mommy. "But I am most thankful for you and your brothers and Daddy."

"Mommy, I am thankful for all of you too!" Sydney said happily.

"Well, that's good!" said Mommy.

"But, Mommy, you forgot about the butterflies and the kitties and the popcorn! And you especially cannot forget about the unicorns!"

"I could never forget about the unicorns," whispered Mommy. "Good night, sweet girl."

About the Author

Sarah Dienethal has a last name that is very hard to pronounce, so give yourself a pat on the back for giving it a good try. She is also the mother of four awesome kids, one being a unicorn- and kitten-loving four-year-old. When she isn't busy picking up the stuffed animals and Legos that cover her floors, threatening her feet at every step, she is trying her best to raise kindhearted, God-loving children. She hopes this book is a good reminder to focus on the little things. So go befriend a butterfly and pray from your heart.